D0513136

Light a Candle for Rosie

Doreen Fiol

Raider Publishing International

New York   London   Swansea

© 2007 Doreen Fiol

All rights reserved. No part of this book may be reproduced stored in a retrieval system or transmitted in any form by any means with out the prior written permission of the publisher, except by a reviewer who may quote brief passages in a review to be printed in a newspaper, magazine or journal.

First Printing

The views, content and descriptions in this book do not represent the views of Raider Publishing International. Some of the content may be offensive to some readers and they are to be advised. Objections to the content in this book should be directed towards the author and owner of the intellectual property rights as registered with their local government.

ISBN: 1-934360-31-7
Published By Raider Publishing International
www.RaiderPublishing.com
New York   London   Swansea

Printed in the United States of America and the United Kingdom
By Lightning Source Ltd.

Light a Candle for Rosie

Doreen Fiol

Chapter One

Rosie Jones sat on the long, low wall swinging one leg rhythmically forward and back, forward and back, the heel of her buckled brown sandal thudding dully against the red brick. The few passers-by did not even glance her way.

"You'd think they couldn't even see me," she muttered, poking her tongue out at the retreating backs of two children who had ignored her smiling 'Hello'. Tossing her mousy bobbed hair out of her eyes she adjusted the tortoiseshell slide that held it in place and looked around her.

The place certainly had changed since she'd seen it last! Gone was the house where she'd lived with Mum, Dad and little Terry and Johnny - along with the whole row of little houses. She closed her eyes and saw them, all the same, with eleven hearth-stoned steps going up to each front door, and railings, and steps leading down to the basement. Swivelling round she looked balefully at the giant tower block that had replaced them.

And where was the corner shop, with its peeling green paint and the sign with letters missing, where Mrs. Green had sold them lollies and black-jacks and gob-stoppers so enormous you could hardly get your mouth round them?

How long had she been away? Surely it couldn't have been that long? She wished her memory wasn't so patchy. Perhaps when she was stronger it would improve and she would be able to piece everything together. Nothing seemed to make sense at the moment.

She remembered her last birthday - her eleventh - well enough. Here, on this very spot, she had sat on her steps waiting for the postman, hoping there would be a card from Dad. How sad she had been when the card didn't arrive. And there was another sadness - something she could almost remember - but it stayed just out of reach of her probing thoughts.

Swinging her legs over the wall, her back to the street, she studied the flats. A group of teenagers came out, laughing and jostling each other. A woman passed them carrying a large box of groceries. She called to one of the boys who took the box from her. Closing the boot of her car she accompanied the boy. Rosie watched as they entered the concrete walkway and disappeared. The group waited for the boy to return. As he emerged they turned impatiently.

"Come on, mate - we'll be late."

"Race yer," he replied, running and leaping the wall inches from Rosie.

"Bloomin' 'ell!" Rosie spluttered, wobbling. "What's the matter wiv yer? You blind or somefink?" Rude lot - could've said sorry, she complained to herself when they didn't bother to answer.

'It don't 'arf look well-off round 'ere now,' she mused. 'All that shopping...and those posh clothes. And all the flats 'ave got lovely curtains.' She swivelled round to face the road again. 'And all them cars! I never seen so many cars!'

Jumping down from the wall she smoothed out her thin flowered dress and started to walk along the road. Turning the corner she could see the main road just ahead.

'It even sounds different,' she thought, waiting to cross. A police car and an ambulance raced by, their sirens blaring. Rosie jumped and stepped back, treading on the toes of a woman behind her.

"Sorry," she said. The woman ignored her.

"I'm sorry," she said, louder. "You see, I got scared - that noise..." Confused and embarrassed, Rosie stopped. The woman was not even listening.

"Oh, blow yer then!" muttered Rosie rudely, only under her breath. Once across the busy road they turned in different directions, the woman towards the Portobello Market, Rosie towards the big iron railway bridge, the canal and the Halfpenny Steps.

The Halfpenny Steps led down from the canal bridge to the little streets below. Rosie breathed a sigh of relief. Thank Goodness! Here nothing had changed. The little two-storey terraced houses with their net curtains were just as she remembered: except that the house that had been her gran's now had a big brass horse in the window instead of the treasured aspidistra.

She crossed the road and peered through the railings at her old school. The playground was deserted, but heads, sometimes grouped, sometimes singly, bobbed in and out of view as they passed the windows. One or two looked out. Rosie waved, but no-one waved back. Perhaps the teacher has her eye on them, Rosie thought. A boy and a girl about Rosie's age came out of the main door. They each carried a bag. Starting at opposite ends of the playground they began to collect the empty crisp bags and sweet wrappers that whirled and skimmed and scurried in the soft summer breeze. When it was clear that they were not going to speak to her Rosie moved on.

Next to the school stood the church. Rosie hesitated before turning the black ring-handle and pushing open the heavy door. She had not been inside since Gran's funeral. Mum and Terry and Johnny had been with her then.

Inside was dark and cool, the dimness relieved to one side of the altar by a dozen or so candles burning in a wrought-iron stand in front of a statue of the Virgin Mary. Slowly she made her way along the aisle towards the flickering lights. 'Each one represents someone's prayers,' her mother had told her. She would have liked to put one up now, but she had no coppers to put in the black box on the stand.

A lady entered through the side door and started to arrange flowers on the main altar. A man came in and sat near Rosie, his head in his hands. A young foreign-looking priest walked across to check the oil in the Sanctuary light. Nobody took any notice of Rosie.

Coming out into the daylight she blinked and shivered. It had been chilly in the church. Pulling her cardigan across her chest she went up the Halfpenny Steps to Ladbroke Grove. In the distance she could hear more police cars or ambulances, their strange new sound startling her ears.

Somewhere in the back of her mind she thought she could hear bells clanging, and horses hooves. She wished she could remember. And she wished someone would speak to her. Or just smile at her, notice she was there.

'There's a mystery here somewhere,' she told herself, 'and no mistake!'

Chapter Two

Reaching what had once been her own street, Rosie sat herself back on the wall, pushing her heel into a loose brick to give herself a lift-up. She did not feel at all well; she felt peculiar, as if she had just recovered from 'flu, or were waking from a bad dream.

A fat lady and two children came around the corner. Rosie watched them, idly at first, then with more interest as they talked and pointed in her direction. Perhaps they were coming to talk to her? The lady fumbled in her handbag for her handkerchief and dabbed at her eyes. The children turned her gently around and the three of them walked away.

"Bovver!" said Rosie, who was lonely and bored. A little black dog wandered along the pavement. "'Ere boy! 'Ere! Come on!" The dog stopped a moment, turned his head towards her, then backed away.

"Come on, silly. I'm not goin' ter 'urt yer." Rosie jumped down and went towards him, making coaxing noises. The dog snarled and bared his teeth. Rosie was cross, but surprised too. She loved animals and they usually loved her.

Animals. Something to do with an animal...

Again something that was almost a memory troubled her.

"Oh alright - if you're goin' ter be so unfriendly..." She turned away and climbed back on the wall. The dog, hackles still raised, passed on, stepping into the gutter to keep well away from her.

The boy and girl were back, alone this time, and making their way towards her. By now Rosie was used to people taking no notice of her so she was startled when the girl smiled and spoke.

"Hello!" Her voice had a soft country sound.

"'Ello."

"D'you live here?" asked the boy, scrambling up beside her.

"No - not now - I used to."

"So you're just visiting, like us," said the girl, sitting beside Rosie.

"Yes - visiting. I've been away - ill."

"We're on holiday with our grandma and grandfather," the boy volunteered. "We're staying in a flat in Ladbroke Grove - down near the station."

"On 'oliday? But it's a schoolday."

"Yes, it is really. But Nan and Grandpa have come up to look after our aunt's flat in Ladbroke Grove while she's gone abroad. Scared of burglars our Aunt Ann is - got the place all locked up and barred. It's like a prison to get out, let alone get in!"

"My brother's exaggerating of course," the girl laughed. "But it's true she didn't want to leave the flat empty so we've come up for the week - nine days really. Our school said it was alright."

"We've got work to do while we're here though. Research." The boy pulled a face. "I think a holiday should be a proper holiday." The girls nodded in agreement.

"What's yer names?" Rosie asked.

"Bethan Trevalyn - and this is Joshua - Beth and Josh. What's yours?"

"Rosie. Rose-Marie Bernadette Jones."
They smiled at each other.

"You don' 'arf talk funny, where d'yer come from?"

"Cornwall," Beth and Josh both answered together.

"Is that country?"

"Yes - very!" Beth laughed. "Lots of fields and hills..."

"If you're not going up one, you're goin' down one." Josh put in.

"And hens and sheep and cattle."

"And cow-pats!"

"Trust you to think of those!"

"Well - I'm always stepping in 'em!"

They jumped down from the wall. Walking along, glad of each others' company, they chatted happily.

"You said you used to live here. Where?" asked Bethan.

"Here in this street."

"So did our grandma!"

"My granny used ter live over that way," Rosie's arm waved to the left. "Over by the cut."

"The cut?"

"The canal - over the 'A'penny steps."

Bethan had not been very impressed with London so far. Apart from the museums and the Tower and Buckingham Palace - and they could only afford one trip to these - it had all seemed noisy and dreary.

Joshua had found it much more fun, the highlight being riding up and down on the escalators in the underground stations. To Bethan the Apeney Steps and a canal sounded exciting.

"Can you take us?" she asked Rosie

"I've just bin over there; but alright, come on."

"Your grandma doesn't live there any more then?" Beth wished she hadn't asked as Rosie, until then so cheerful, looked suddenly sad.

"No."

"Where's she gone? Moved away?" Josh persisted.

"She's dead."

"Oh! When did she...?" Beth stopped Josh's questioning with a sharp poke and a frown. Why did he have to know everything about everything? Couldn't he see the girl was upset?

"Look - if you'd rather not go..."

"It's alright," she smiled. Joshua, never one to be squashed for long, began to talk about the research they must do.

"About the war?" Rosie sounded troubled.

"Yes - you know - World War Two. 'Course it was ages ago. History really. But as most of us know someone who was alive in it, our school thought it would be interesting to find out about it first hand," Bethan explained.

"Our Nan and Grandpa were children then.

Nan lived where we met you; when it was all little houses, though, not great tower blocks - those have only been up the last thirty years or so."

"How - how long ago was the war?" Rosie's voice was quiet and shaky.

"More than fifty years," said Joshua proudly, pleased that he knew. Rosie, whose steps had been getting slower and slower, stopped.

"What's the matter?" Beth asked.

"Nothing. I don't know." Rosie's voice was almost a whisper. "I've got to go back." Turning away from them she began to retrace her steps.

"Wait! Please - we don't have to go where you don't want - we didn't mean to upset you."

They walked in silence back the way they had come. From time to time Bethan and Joshua looked at each other, then at the girl. Her head was slightly bowed, her face had a shut-in look and her feet dragged a little as she walked. Beth noticed the cotton dress with the little flowers all over it, and the puff-sleeves and peter-pan collar. Old-fashioned, like the one Nan was wearing in an old photo. She felt pleased about the comfortable track-suits and trainers she and her brother were wearing.

Still in silence they came to the corner. Uncertain whether to continue with Rosie or to go on back to the flat, they stopped.

"D'you think she wants us?" Josh whispered.

"Don't know," Beth glanced at Rosie standing a little apart.

"Rosie..." she said gently, hesitantly. "Rosie..."

There was no response. Beth, a little hurt, withdrew her outstretched hand. Josh shrugged.

"Oh well!" he muttered. With a last puzzled look at the impassive figure of the girl who had been so friendly such a short time ago, they turned away.

"Beth... Josh," her voice, still quiet, sounded strange as if it came from a long way away.

"Yes Rosie?"

"You said your gran lived around 'ere... in... the war?"

"Yes - that's right. She was nine when it began. She was sent to Cornwall -evacuated. That's why she cried when she saw her old street. People she knew -children - were killed - in the bombing. She had a best friend - she won't talk about her, but Grandpa told us..."

"Your gran - what was - is - her name?"

17

"Louise Trevalyn!"

"No. I mean before she was married. When she was a girl - my age - in the war."

"I don't know. I'll ask her." Beth wondered if perhaps Nan and Rosie's gran had known each other.

"But... it is Louise?" Rosie was looking at her so intently that Bethan felt uncomfortable and shifted from one foot to the other.

"Yes - Louise."

"But everyone - all her friends, and Grandpa - all call her 'Wee'." Joshua giggled as he always did at the thought of his large, treble-chinned grandma being called 'Wee'. And of course there was the other meaning!

Bethan explained. "She's always been called 'Wee' in the family because when she was little..."

"She couldn't say Louise," finished Rosie.

"That's right." Bethan laughed. "I suppose it's easy to guess."

But Rosie didn't laugh. She looked at them, especially at Bethan, long and hard. Then without another word to them, she left them. They watched until she disappeared around the corner.

"I heard her say 'Wee' under her breath," said Joshua. "Wee Ashwood!"

"So did I," said Bethan. "As if she were - you know - remembering something."

Puzzled, they went back to the flat for tea.

"Louise Ashwood. 'Wee' Ashwood." Rosie stood looking up at the flats, repeating the name over and over again. The tears ran unchecked down her deathly pale face. Of course everything looked strange, sounded strange! Time mattered here -and it had been a long time. A long, long time. She remembered now! She wasn't fuzzie-headed after 'flu. She hadn't been ill. Suddenly she could see everything clearly. The place she had been: the knowledge that she could not go on until she found out...found out what? That bit she still couldn't remember. That's where she needed help - why she had answered the call.

"Rosie! Ro..s..ie!" She heard the call and looked around her, but could see nothing through the thick blanket of mist.

"Rosie!"

There it was again. The voice had a strange, eerie quality, seeming to come from a great distance. It echoed all around her and she hesitated, unsure which direction to take. There were other voices now, clamouring.

"Don't go! Stay! Stay with us!"

She ignored them, peering over and around the vague shapes, trying to pin-point the sound.

Someone was calling her! Someone knew her name! Maybe they could help her get out of this dreadful place where nobody knew anybody. Nobody belonged. She had not heard her name for so long.

"I must go," she said, shrugging off the hands which tried to hold her. Long fingers dug into her, limbs wound around her legs as she moved slowly, steathily into the darkness. Now the voices all around her grew louder, filling her head. The shadows pulled at her more determindly. Perhaps she had imagined it. Perhaps there had been no call... She almost allowed herself to be pulled back amongst them.

"Rosie!" Louder now, clearer.

"I must go," she said again.

Resolutely she stepped forward. The mouth of the tunnel yawned before her.

Then it was sucking her in, dragging her, whirling and twirling, towards the light at the other end...

Leaning against the chest-high wall, burying her face in her arms, she sobbed. People passed, almost touching her - she didn't bother about them.

She knew they couldn't see her.

Chapter Three

"You must have seen her, Nan! She was sitting on the wall right where you said your house used to be."

The children had been recounting the events of the afternoon and could not believe their grandmother had not even noticed the child who had been watching them so intently.

"Maybe it's because I was so upset," their grandmother reasoned. "I'm sorry about that. I was quite overcome - remembering. Especially.." she stopped and busied herself clearing the table.

"Especially?" Beth prompted.

"Nothing dear - just a stupid fancy," she paused, frowning. "You see, for a moment - just a moment - I did imagine there was someone there - like a girl I used to know..."

"There! You did see her," Joshua exclaimed. "I knew you couldn't have not seen her!"

"Of course Nan couldn't have not seen her," Bethan pointed out, correcting him as usual.

"That's what's called a double..."

"Nan knows what I mean," Josh grumbled sulkily. Why did Beth have to be such a know-all!

"Anyway," Nan intervened briskly, hoping to stop the quarrel that looked like flaring up. "It was not your young friend, for when I looked again there was no-one there. "Now," she said, dismissing the subject, "Let's go and see what Grandpa's up to."

Later that night, long after the living noises had stopped around them and the lights of neighbouring flats had gone out one by one, the children talked.

Huddled together in one of the twin beds, their whispering lost to all but each other in the big comfortable duvet, they went over and over the strange happenings of the day.

Long-fingered shadows from the street lamps changed shape on the walls, breaking and rejoining as lights from passing cars sputtered amongst them. Here and there a door banged, followed by loud 'sshs!' As the night wore on the traffic lessened but did not stop completely. Joshua fell asleep, cuddled against Bethan. She eased herself away, careful not to wake him, and crossed the room to the other bed. Nobody slept with

Joshua! Not even when they had a houseful, like at Christmas. Dad, who had tried once, said it was like going fifteen rounds with a champion heavyweight boxer!

Standing at the window, the summer sky just beginning to lighten, she peered along the road. She could just see the corner where they had parted from Rosie. Where was she now? Why had she left them like that? And had their grandmother seen her, and if so...? We've talked about it nearly all night, she thought, and it's till a puzzle. Perhaps they would meet her again. She hoped so. She had liked the strange, quiet girl. A milk float purred along the road, stopped, and after a brief clatter of crates and bottles, went on. Bethan realized it was morning already and, as if to confirm it, an alarm went off somewhere nearby. A shaft of light from the next door window made her blink. Chilled and very tired she climbed into bed.

The sound of footsteps running downstairs filtered through the wall; a door banged, then a car door, followed by the sound of the engine. Bethan was suddenly homesick. She missed the birds' early-morning song, the old rooster shouting his noisy greeting. She missed the cat, who, if she hadn't been caught, would have cuddled up on her feet, and the old dog asleep on the landing, whimpering now and then, no doubt dreaming of chasing rabbits.

But most of all she missed Mum and Dad. She was surprised to feel a tear on her cheek. She had really looked forward to this holiday; it had sounded wonderfully exciting. But now, well, what had they done? Visited a few museums, including the war museum because of their project, seen the Palace, which secretly she didn't think looked much like a Palace, heard her grandmother exclaim over things that were much changed or, with equal amazement, over things that hadn't changed at all. And met a girl who might be her friend - but who she may never see again.

'Well, you must not let Nan and Grandpa know you are disappointed,' she told herself finally. Wiping away the tear, and those which had followed it, she turned over and went to sleep.

Grandpa's voice asking them if they were going to lie there until they grew moss, woke them. They sat up sleepily rubbing their eyes. Joshua was the first to notice the smell of toast and was out of bed and running to the kitchen.

"Hold on young man," *Grandpa stopped him with a firm hand on his head.* "You won't starve! Bathroom first!"

What made grown-ups so crazy on washing, Josh wanted to know. He'd had a bath before he went to bed, for goodness sake! And anyway, you only got dirty again. He didn't mind cleaning his teeth, he liked the taste of toothpaste, and he didn't want bad teeth like his friend David had - but couldn't he have done them after breakfast? Grumbling, clutching his stomach and murmuring about cruelty to children, Joshua stumbled into his least favourite place.

Bethan got up more slowly and made both beds while waiting for her brother to finish in the bathroom. She smiled to herself knowing he would not be washing 'properly' but just splashing the water to make it sound good. So far their grandparents had not inspected his ears and the backs of neck and legs as their mother did at home. She wondered what state he would be in when they got back. There was still most of the week to go. Her homesickness of the previous night forgotten she felt a thrill of excitement. As they had slept so late Nan had decided to postpone her intended West End shopping trip. The children could have the day to themselves. Joshua whooped with delight; he hated shopping almost as much as he hated washing.

"Will you be alright, you two? You won't be bored?" Nan asked anxiously.

"No, Nan, we'll be fine," Bethan assured her. "We've got things we want to do!"

26

"She wants to see if we can find Rosie again," Joshua explained, his mouth full of toast.

"Rosie?" Nan sounded sharp. The children looked up wondering what they had done wrong.

"Yes - Rosie. The girl we told you about yesterday - the one you saw - didn't see, by your old house...where your old house used to be." Bethan spoke quickly, nervously, as she always did when she was worried. What was the matter with Nan?

"Rosie? Rosie who?" asked Nan.

"Rosie Jones - Rose-Marie Bernadette Jones. Oh, by the way, she asked us to ask you your name - Louise what - before you married Grandpa."

"Tell her..." Nan stumbled, took a deep breath. "Tell her - Louise Ashwood - Wee Ashwood."

Bethan and Joshua looked at each other in shocked surprise. Joshua choked, spraying toast across the table. Grandpa thumped him on the back, reproving him for cramming his mouth too full. Nan didn't even notice. She was staring at the wall, as if the wall was no longer there and she could see a long, long way over the roof-tops. And under her breath, in the same sort of voice as Rosie had used when she left them yesterday, she was repeating "Rosie Jones... Rosie Jones..."

Chapter Four

Rosie sat on the wall and shivered. It was always colder near somewhere she had lived, she realized; here, over the Ha'penny steps by Gran's house, in the church. Coming and going was a warm, tingly, electrical sensation, contrasting sharply with the chill of arrival. She pulled her old cardigan closely around her, and chuckled, thinking of the lady whose toes she had trodden on the previous day. It could be fun, knowing you couldn't be seen. But Bethan and Joshua could see her. She wondered why. 'Good job they can,' she thought. 'Otherwise I'd be all on my own here, with no-one to help.'

But could they help? How could she explain to them when she didn't understand herself? How do you tell someone you are a ghost and you've come back because you have something to do - but you don't know what it is? She could imagine how she would have reacted! The finger-to-the-head crazy sign, a giggle with whoever was willing to share the joke - and off quick!

Supposing she wasn't there when they arrived (if they arrived) and then materialized in front of them? No, tempting as the idea was, the shock would probably send them running back, screaming, along Ladbroke Grove. Perhaps she should sound them out first, find out how they felt about ghosts. Yes, that would be best. But perhaps they won't come, she thought. After all, they had made no arrangements to meet again. But they had! She had asked Bethan to find out her grandmother's name - that was like telling them she wanted to see them again, wasn't it? Considerably cheered, Rosie waited, watching the corner.

It was a long wait. At first she amused herself by making faces and poking her tongue out at passers-by. Then she picked up a stone and plopped it immediately behind a lady, who thought she had dropped something and spent ages looking for it. A crusty-looking elderly gentleman was her next victim. As he mumbled and 'hurrumped' his way past her Rosie picked up a leaf and tickled his nose. He brushed his hand across his face. Rosie tickled his ear. 'Drat these flies,' he grumbled, waving his arms. Rosie danced around him brushing his ears, his nose, his whiskery chin with the leaf. He moved faster, swishing and tap-tapping his walkingstick. The 'fly' followed. Helpless with laughter Rosie stood aside as the man and Beth and Josh, who had just entered the street, collided. Joshua sat down heavily on the pavement. The man, winded, breathed out a word the children were sure they were not supposed to hear...and definitely would not be allowed to say. Joshua, scrambling to his feet and rubbing his bottom, stored it in the back of his mind. It would be a good one for playground 'swaps' when he got back to school.

"Well, you young hooligans?" The man had got his breath back and was glaring at them. He sounded very cross.

"Well what?" Bethan asked politely.

"Well what! Well what! I'll give you 'well what'!" He raised his stick threateningly. "You come racing round the corner nearly knocking me flying - and you ask 'well what'? Don't you even say you're sorry?"

"Excuse me," Joshua said, eyeing the waving stick warily. "But you bumped into us."

"Perhaps we should all say sorry," Bethan said quickly, seeing the man go red in the face.

"Well - er - hurrumph..."

"It was my fault," Rosie joined them, giggling. "I'm the one who should say sorry!"

"Hello! We wondered if you would come." Neither Bethan nor Joshua had noticed Rosie, and were really pleased to see

her. They both grinned broadly. The man looked from one to the other, bewildered.

"You wondered if I'd come? Do I know you? I'm sure I don't! Make a point of not knowing anyone with children - or anyone at all, if I can help it!"

"No - not you - her."

He followed Joshua's pointing finger and looked crosser than ever.

"Look, mister, we're very sorry, we all crashed into each other. Nobody's hurt." Beth grabbed her brother.

"My bum is," he rubbed it again.

The man went on his way muttering about flies, and children in general, and the children of to-day in particular.

"I thought he was going to whack us with his stick," Bethan sighed with relief as the man disappeared from view.

"So did I - and I'm bruised already!"

Rosie smiled at them "I wouldn't have let him," she assured them.

Serious now, the children looked at Rosie.

"I'm sure you wouldn't," said Bethan quietly.

Rosie looked doubtful for a moment, then took a deep breath. "Did you notice that he...?" She stopped.

"Couldn't see you?" finished Bethan. "Yes, we noticed." The silence seemed to go on a long time, then... "So, you know?" Rosie hung her head as she asked the question that was no longer a question. She was afraid to look at them.

"Yes - we know. We thought there was something strange about you yesterday. Then, after talking to our Nan, I put two and two together..."

"Making twenty-two," quipped Joshua, never one to miss an opportunity to be funny. "If they're side by side!" The girls ignored him.

"Especially," Bethan continued, "when our Nan went so peculiar over your name. And I do believe she saw you - just she won't admit it. By the way, she said to tell you 'Louise Ashwood' - 'Wee' Ashwood."

"I know," said Rosie.

"Then - just now - well, it was clear that he couldn't see you - and we could -so that means you're a - a..."

Bethan couldn't quite bring herself to use the word.

"Ghost." Rosie said it. There! It was out now. "It's alright, it still feels strange for me too. I only realized meself after I left you."

"You mean you didn't know you're a ghost?" Joshua was fascinated. "You were going around like normal, talking and everything?" He paused a moment, thinking. "Do you think we could be ghosts and don't know it yet?"

The girls laughed. "No, silly!"

"There would be lots of fings what puzzle yer - what don't fit," explained Rosie.

"Everything puzzles me," Joshua persisted, making them laugh again.

"Well - I can assure you we are not ghosts," Bethan squeezed his arm affectionately.

"But Rosie is?"

"Yes - Rosie is."

"Why? Why are you a ghost, Rosie?"

"Yes, Rosie. Why?"

"I don't know - that's what I was 'opin' you'd 'elp me find out." She lifted her head and looked at her two friends. "Oh, I'm so glad you know! I bin tryin' to think of 'ow to tell yer!" She explained about her rejected plan to materialize in front of them.

"Coo! Could you really?" Joshua's eyes shone with excitement. "I'd love to see you do that!"

"Well - p'raps I will - sometime." Rosie half-promised, not entirely sure she could manage it at will. So far she had only appeared twice, yesterday and today, neither occasion requiring any deliberate effort on her part. And going, after leaving the children yesterday, had needed no conscious decision either. She had just drifted off, back into the mist, almost into the tunnel. She had heard - vaguely, a long way away - the whispering, echoing voices of the shadow-people, had imagined their arms lengthening, writhing like snakes towards her, trying to pull her back. But she was not going back. She would find out - she MUST find out - what it was she needed to know - then she could go on.

So she had fought the pull of the swirling mist and remained close to the wall, waiting for the time to reappear.

"We wouldn't have been scared, would we Beth?" Joshua was saying.

"Well, we might have been, if we weren't expecting it," Bethan answered honestly. "But not now," she added, smiling at Rosie.

Rosie grinned back and told them about the fun she'd had just before they had turned up.

"Ooh! That was really wicked!" Joshua laughed, delighting in such naughtiness. "Wish we'd been here earlier, I'd have loved to have seen him dancing around and waving his stick and flapping his hands! I bet he looked like an old crow!"

They strolled along, laughing, to the place they wordlessly agreed was their spot. Bethan levered herself up on the wall using her hands and the back of her heel.

"But seriously Rosie, I don't suppose you've come back just to play tricks on old miseries, have you?"

Rosie frowned. "No." She jumped up beside Bethan. Joshua scrambled up, jumping forward and swinging one leg over to sit astride, facing the girls.

"Why then?" Joshua privately thought that playing tricks on people was a perfectly good reason.

At Rosie's quietly repeated "I...don't...know," Bethan looked at the other girl's sad, troubled face. She reached out an arm, as if to put it around Rosie's shoulders, hesitated, then withdrew it. She'd read somewhere about people trying to touch ghosts and their hands passing right through them. She didn't think she would like that.

Chapter Six

'Wee' Trevalyn sat very still, her plump hands gripping the red notebook. She had listened very carefully to the children's story and was trying to think of sensible things to say, like 'what fantastic imaginations you children have' or 'let's go somewhere interesting and get all this ghost nonsense out of your heads.'

But how could she, when, despite all her commonsense, and all the arguments she could think up, she half believed them?

Bethan watched her struggling with herself and signalled to Joshua. They went into the kitchen.

"Let's make a cup of tea," she said, filling the kettle. "Give her a chance to think by herself!"

Returning to the sitting room, with three cups of tea and a plate of biscuits on a tray, they sat down, both feeling very apprehensive. Bethan wondered why they were. After all, they hadn't done anything wrong.

"We haven't made it up - honest Nan!" Joshua blurted out, showing that he was thinking along the same lines.

"No dears, I'm sure you haven't."

Bethan and Joshua looked at each other. She believed them! Bethan took a deep breath. "Nan, we've got to help Rosie. She's here - she's come back. But she doesn't know why. We must help her find out, so she can...so she can..." she hesitated, stumbling.

"Be dead," said Joshua, matter-of-factly.

"Rest," said Nan. She sipped her tea, looking through the wall again. Suddenly brisk, she rose to her feet, knocking the tray and tipping over the fortunately empty cups. Funny, the children thought, Nan wasn't usually clumsy.

"Right! Now!" She picked up the notebook which had fallen to the floor. "Let's see what we've got. She chewed her lip for a moment or two. "I think first of all we need to know if Rosie's alright. Oh, dear! That doesn't sound quite right, does it? But you know what I mean."

"Yes. We're worried - she just sort of... faded away. We'll go first thing in the morning. Oh I do hope she'll be there!" Bethan felt it was desperately important to see her friend again. Supposing they'd lost her - made her go away for good? "Where would she go, Nan, if she can't - you know - be properly at rest?"

"I don't know, Beth," Nan admitted. "But she was my best friend, and I loved her - so if there is a way to help her then I'm quite sure we must find it."

"We? Are you coming in on this, Nan?"

"I don't know about 'coming in on it', Joshua. She is still a child - Beth's age - and I am now a middle-aged lady." The children had never heard their grandmother refer to getting old before. "Maybe that's why she chose you instead," she added.

"How did she know we were coming?"

"That's something else I don't know," Nan turned away from Joshua and fiddled with the tray, standing the tipped-over cups back on their saucers.

"There's an awful lot we don't know," grumbled Joshua petulantly. "After all, if she can't tell us what she wants how can we do anything about it? I think it's going to get a bit boring, her going all quiet, and disappearing and things. P'raps we ought to leave her to sort it out for herself. Then we could go to the park tomorrow - we've only got a couple of days left and..."

"No!" Bethan turned on him sharply. "No! We're going to help her! We are!" She glared at her brother. Joshua looked sulkier than ever, he didn't like being shouted at.

"Well - it's stupid! How can you help a ghost? A stupid, stupid ghost what doesn't even know why it's ghosting! Why can't it be a proper ghost anyway? All white, with chains, or it's head off, or something. I wouldn't mind that! At least it wouldn't be boring! This one's no fun!" Joshua sat down hard, folded his arms, pushed his chin on to his chest and scrunched himself into a bad-tempered, scowling lump. "Anyway," he said, not looking up. "I'm not coming."

"In that case Bethan and I will have to do the detective-work on our own," said Nan reasonably. "Pity, I thought you might have liked that. You're usually good at getting answers to questions."

Warily interested, Joshua lifted one eyebrow, being careful to keep the other one frowning. He looked up. "What d'you mean?"

39

Nan explained. Next morning, after they had checked on Rosie, of course, she would take them to Kensal Green cemetery. If they could find the grave they would then have the date of Rosie's death.

"I know it was in May," said Nan. "My mother wrote and told me. A direct hit, she said, about 3 o'clock in the morning. Rosie and her mum and her two brothers, all..." her lip trembled.

Bethan put her arm around her Nan's ample waist. She couldn't reach right round, but she was sure it was a comfort just the same. Nan swallowed hard.

"Her father - Uncle Eddie I called him - had been killed in action a couple of months or so before."

"What about Billy? Is he dead too?" Joshua thought it might improve things if there was a boy ghost.

Nan shook her head, saying she couldn't add anything to what Rosie had already told them, except that he would be over sixty if he was still alive. Joshua wondered if they could track him down. Nan didn't think that was very likely considering the job his step-father had done. With all the developing and building in London they would have moved long ago, she was sure. Joshua's interest flagged again and he went into the sitting-room to watch the telly and wait for tea.

40

Chapter Seven

Bethan felt strange sitting on the wall on her own. She had been unable to persuade Josh to come; he had gone with Grandpa to Kensington Gardens. Grandpa had been surprised when Bethan and Nan had refused the outing. He had thought that the lure of the model boats on the Round Pond, and the Peter Pan statue would be impossible to resist.

Bethan looked at her watch. Ten o'clock. She had been here an hour already. If Rosie didn't turn up soon she would be too late. Nan was meeting her on the corner at half-past.

Several people strolling past in the bright May sunshine eyed her curiously. Bethan fidgeted, embarrassed. Why didn't Rosie come? Surely they hadn't frightened her away? 'Oh please Rosie! Please,' she pleaded silently, screwing her eyes up tight, willing her friend to come. Opening her eyes hopefully, expectantly, she looked up and down the street, then swivelled round to look along the straight concrete paths between the tower blocks. No sign of Rosie. Sighing, Bethan checked the time again. Ten-twenty-five. Reluctantly she got down and started to walk towards the corner. Every few steps she stopped and looked back. Perhaps she hadn't looked properly? Perhaps Rosie was, sort of, vague - not very clear. After all, yesterday they had seen her fade before their eyes. Running all the way back she peered around into the clear, empty air.

"What yer lookin' for, luv?" A lady asked kindly.

"Er - nothing. No-one. It's alright - I'm meeting my grandmother." Bethan, flustered, went hurriedly back to the corner.

"She didn't come then." It was more a statement than a question as Louise Trevalyn looked at her grand-daughter's solemn face.

"No, Nan. What do you think can have happened to her?"

"It's no good us guessing, Beth. We neither of us know much about this. I think we should do as we suggested - find out the date of her death, if we can. That could give us a starting point."

"And then?"

"Let's take it a step at a time shall we? First the cemetery. My dear parents are buried there, too, so it will be something of a pilgrimage. I remembered to bring their cards, so I have the grave number." From her handbag she took out two yellowing, black-edged cards, the first bearing the text 'Till the day breaks and the shadows flee away.' The second 'Through the mists, united for ever.' Both bore the same grave number.

"We can get a bus in Harrow Road - take us right to the cemetery gates," Nan was saying, putting the cards carefully back in their envelope.

Until they were past the canal bridge and the Halfpenny Steps Bethan was silent, remembering the last time she had come this way, with Rosie.

"I wonder if...?"

"Do you think she might...?" They both spoke at once.

"I suppose it wouldn't hurt to look. I used to go with her to her granny's sometimes. And I went to her school once to see a nativity play."

"You didn't go to the same school then?"

"No. Rosie's family were Catholics. She and her brothers went to the little school you'll see at the bottom of these steps. Here we are - just around the corner. There! Right next to the church."

Bethan looked around her. Here was a little bit of the London her grandmother had often talked about. The narrow street; slim, tight little houses, squeezed together like children with their hands straight at their sides. Painted or polished front doors, white net curtains. A plant or brass ornament in the front room window. Then the church, the school, and a pub; and a paper shop on the opposite corner. Two portly ladies were gossiping in their doorways, one leaning on a broom. Another lady two doors down was cleaning her ground-floor window, throwing in a cheerful comment here and there. A small child, watched by the lady with the broom, rode his tricycle up and down the pavement.

As Louise Trevalyn and Bethan entered the street the occupants looked at them with open curiosity.

'It's just like a village,' Bethan thought. 'A tiny village hiding itself away.'

They stood outside the church, wondering whether to go in or not, aware of several pairs of eyes watching them.

"Have you ever been inside, Nan?" Bethan had turned the handle and the door had opened slightly inwards giving a glimpse of welcome dimness.

"Yes - twice. The first time was when Rosie made her first Communion."

"What's that?"

"It's a special day for Catholic children, when they receive the Communion bread for the first time. I remember it clearly. June, it was. Rosie and I were seven, Billy nine. We were invited as we always played together.

44

Rosie was all in white, with a veil, and flowers in her hair. She was a plain little girl, but that day she looked beautiful. I remember being very jealous and wishing we had something like that. Then Billy kept muttering 'here comes the bride, all fat and wide' and we both got the giggles - and a firm poke in the ribs from Rosie's mother!"

Bethan laughed; she could just imagine it! Pushing the door open they stepped into an enveloping coolness. For a moment or two, coming from the glare into the darkness, they couldn't see properly and their eyes played tricks with shapes and shadows. They slipped into the back pew and sat down.

"You said you'd been in here twice, Nan." Bethan prompted, whispering.

"That's right," Mrs. Trevalyn whispered back, looking around her thoughtfully. "After her grandma's funeral - we came here on our own. Rosie wanted to put up a candle for her. For her to rest in peace. Over there - look. The candle-stand is still there. That's another practice I rather envied - although I never quite understood what it was for. A sign of your prayer going to God, Rosie said. When you left the church your prayer still carried on."

"Should we...?"

Her grandmother, knowing what she was about to ask, shook her head. "I think, if she were able to rest in peace, she would have done so by now. There's something stopping her. And unless we can find out what it is..."

Bethan shivered. "She'll be stuck. Wherever she is, forever! Oh, Nan, we must help her!"

Closing the door firmly behind them, grateful now for the sunshine, they made their way to the cemetery.

Chapter Eight

"Semitry! 'Ere we are, luv. Kensal Green Semitry." The conductor shouted along the bus. "Take yer time, no need ter rush Missus - they ain't goin' nowhere!" He laughed at his own wit, joined by several passengers. Louise Trevalyn thanked him politely, if a little stiffly, and made her way through the press of standing passengers towards the exit. Bethan followed, answering the conductor's broad grin with a friendly smile. She was careful to straighten her face before her grandmother turned to help her off. Nan could be a bit prim - even stuffy at times.

Entering through the imposing iron gates, Bethan looked around her in amazement. Somehow she had expected a small, shady area. Like the one by the church at home, enclosed and sheltered. And quiet, with weathered grey stones and overhanging trees. A place to stroll in and talk quietly, and read a whole family history in a group of headstones. This was enormous!

So open - and so bare! And the tombstones! Hundreds of them! Old ones, new ones, neglected ones, cared-for ones. Gigantic, ostentatious ones - and sad little mounds with no stone at all, only noticeable because of the bumpy ground.

"Oh, Nan." Bethan's voice quivered and held tears. She swallowed hard to stop them reaching her eyes; "We'll never find her. It could take days - weeks." She stopped, and looked again at this vast city of the dead. "Oh Nan," she said again, helplessly.

"Don' 'ee fret, my lover," Nan said, using the Cornish idiom she'd picked up from Grandpa. Bethan responded with a weak smile. With an arm reassuringly around Beth's shoulders Mrs Trevalyn propelled her grand-daughter gently towards what appeared to be an office.

"We'll ask here," she said, taking out the two black-edged cards from her bag. "I know the graves we want will be in the old part of the cemetery but - well, it's been a long time - and so much has changed."

Their enquiry resulted in a roughly drawn map. Referring to this they followed the main path until it branched, then took the left-hand, narrower path which led them to the farthest boundary.

Here there were trees and bushes, and long grass. Beyond the wall they could hear the traffic, sounding further away than it was. There was a cloying, sweet smell of old wood and decaying vegetation and damp dark soil. The sun did not reach here, and despite the warm spring day it was chilly.

"This must be the old part the man told us about," Bethan said, her voice almost a whisper. Her gandmother did not reply. She was walking between the graves, stooping reading the moss-covered names.

"Here we are," she said, kneeling down. Her fingers traced the name 'ALICE ASHWOOD' then followed down, through the dates, to 'CHARLES ASHWOOD' HUSBAND OF THE ABOVE.

"My mother and father. Your great-grandparents. They were nice people, Beth. You would have loved them. And they would have loved you and Josh." Absent-mindedly she began clearing the grass and dead leaves from among the pebbles. Bethan stood quietly, unsure what she should do.

"This won't do," said Mrs Trevalyn suddenly, briskly, helping herself up with one hand on the tombstone and the other on Bethan's arm. "Now - he said a lot of war graves were over to the right."

They moved away and resumed their search. The shadows were lengthening and they were on the point of giving up when Bethan, forgetting where she was for a moment, gave a shout and ran forwards.

"I've found her, Nan! Look - over here." Grabbing a plump arm she pulled and tugged her protesting grandmother through some tangled undergrowth.

"Slow down Beth! I can't keep up with you! Anyway we shouldn't be charging around a graveyard." But she hurried just the same, glad they had at last found what they were looking for.

"See, Nan," Bethan had parted the weeds and flowering grasses covering the small stone.

JONES ELLEN MAY BORN 1907
WIFE OF EDWARD JONES KILLED IN ACTION APRIL 1940
also ROSE-MARIE BERNADETTE AGED 11 years
TERENCE EDWARD AGED 8 years
JOHN DAVID AGED 3 1/2 years
CHILDREN OF THE ABOVE KILLED IN AIR-RAID 10th MAY 1941
UNITED IN LOVE FOREVER

"But Rosie isn't united in love forever! She's out there - somewhere - on her own." Bethan was crying. Louise Trevalyn - Wee Ashwood - fought back her own tears.

"I know dear. She's not safe yet. But she will be. You'll help her. I know you will."

"But - suppose she doesn't come back, Nan?"

50

"She will. Rosie was quite a girl for getting what she wanted."

They stared down again at the chipped grey stone.

"The tenth of May. That's tomorrow," Bethan murmured and a shiver ran through her.

It had happened all those years ago - tonight.

Chapter Nine

The night seemed to be going on forever. Bethan, unable to sleep, sat at the window looking out at the city-lit sky. A tiny sliver of silver hung neatly between the chimney pots. New moon - must make a wish, she thought. At home, with darkness all around, the stars, too, would have been clearly visible. She yawned, but felt too restless to get into bed. Joshua, after his day out, had crashed as soon as his head touched the pillow. A distant clock struck two o'clock. Joshua stirred, thrust his feet over the side of the bed, searching for the floor, and trundled off sleepily along the passage.

"Too much lemonade and ices," he explained on his return. Bethan, remembering the long thirsty hours in the cemetery, felt a momentary pang of jealousy. But she couldn't let herself dwell on a few missed treats; she had more important things to think about.

Joshua dragged the duvet over to the window-seat and they huddled together as

Bethan whispered the events of the day. Joshua had been too tired after tea, and she had felt too sad to talk about it anyway.

"So tonight's her anniversary - a sort of birthday, only..."

"Yes," Bethan interrupted, not wanting to finish it.

"Why don't we go round? See if she's there?"

"What - now? In the middle of the night? Josh, that's crazy!"

"Why not?" Josh, wide awake now, was excited. It would be an adventure! "You said she didn't come this morning - yesterday morning. Ghosts might be able to come out better at night!"

Bethan thought the idea over carefully. It shouldn't be too difficult to get out - they just had to turn the latch and slip off the chain. And the keys were left on the hall table, so getting back in would be no problem either. But what if they got caught? They would be in terrible trouble, she had no doubt. Nan and Grandpa were very patient with their grand-children, but their tolerance would not stretch that far, she was sure! And no-one, by silent mutual consent, had said anything to Grandpa about their ghost-friend, so he would be even angrier than Nan - he couldn't be expected to understand.

Chewing her bottom lip, she weighed up the fors and againsts. Josh could be right - perhaps they could see Rosie. It might be their only chance. Or they could get caught either leaving or re-entering the flat. Or by someone outside, puzzled by two children wandering alone in the dead of night. It would mean straight home, for sure. Whereas if they didn't go they had another few days in which to help Rosie. If they could find her.

"Alright," she said, making up her mind. "But we must be really quiet." They dressed hurriedly, putting their track-suits over their pyjamas. Joshua, liking to do things properly, and having read books on runaways and night-time adventures, put a pillow lengthwise in each bed. "If they do look in they'll think we're fast asleep," he whispered.

Ready, they stood once more at the window. The hard yellow light from the street-lamps gave the houses an unfamiliar look, changing the colours of bricks and doors and curtains, as if the road dressed differently for the night. There was little traffic and the usually busy road looked deserted. Only a lone cat prowled, investigating the dust-bins on the other side. At a nod from Bethan they turned away and crept into the passage. They stopped for a moment outside their grandparents' bedroom, listening to the heavy, steady breathing and the occasional snore. There was a loud snort, and mumbling, and the sound of creaking and heaving as someone turned over.

"That's Nan," whispered Josh, suppressing a giggle.

"Ssh," Bethan warned, finger on lips.

A floor-board creaked under a tip-toeing foot and they stopped again, holding their breath. The expected 'You alright, dear?' didn't come. Bethan popped into the toilet then took a few steps back towards the bedroom, just in case. All quiet. She joined Joshua at the front door, this time avoiding the squeaky board. The chain slipped off easily, and, unlatching the heavy door, the children slipped out, closing it silently behind them with the key. Their soft-soled trainers made no sound as they stole into the night.

Keeping close to the railinged fronts of the houses they dodged behind pillars and into doorways to avoid being spotted from passing cars.

Crossing to the other side of the road proved to be more difficult than they had expected. Every time they tried a car would appear heading their way. Once a police-car cruised by and they scuttled down into a basement, hiding behind some dust-bins. Hearts beating fast, their breath came out in a long, loud sigh when it was safely past. For a moment the road appeared clear again.

"Quick," said Bethan. "Let's run for it! Now!"

They dashed up the steps and across the road.

"Nearly there," Bethan gasped. "It shouldn't be so light in the side-streets."
Rounding the corner they stopped and simultaneously reached for each other's hand.

Open-mouthed, eyes staring, they viewed the scene before them.

Chapter Ten

The moon, no longer a slim segment, shone full and clear and low above them; a huge round disc giving light as bright as day. The whole street was visible, clearer than in daylight; every shape, every line as if drawn by a darker pencil.

And the shapes were different. Gone were the tall oblongs with straight paths between. Gone was the long line of wall on which they had sat with Rosie. In their place, picked out by a patch of extra brightness, as if they were special, was a row of little terraced houses. Triangles of roofs, touching, white steps gleaming, like teeth. Windows, curtained black, like blind eyes. No light gleamed, not from the unlit street-lamps, nor from the houses.

Two men walked, evenly paced, one carrying a heavy torch. The shorter of the two wheezed and stopped to cough from time-to-time. The other man was older and wore thick glasses. Both wore tin hats and carried a bag on one shoulder, and an armband with ARP in black letters. They passed the children without a glance and stopped a few feet away.

"Won't need this tonight, George," the older man said, lifting his torch.

"No - not with that up there," his partner agreed, pointing a thumb at the moon. His companion nodded.

"Give us 'ard time, that will. Jerry's bound to take advantage."

"Bound to. Proper 'bombers' moon' that," they gazed studiously upwards.

"Surprised they 'aven't bin over already. It was non-stop last night from 'alf past seven."

"I know - I was off last night - but could I get any rest? Could I 'eck! What wiv Jerry and me chest..."

He coughed hard and spat. "Perhaps 'e'll give us a miss ternight," he wheezed hopefully.

"Cor blimey! Some 'opes mate! 'E won't miss a chance like this, not wiv that up there to show 'im the way. Docks'll take another bashin' that's for sure - and we'll get any spares."

They stood in companionable silence, broken only by the short man's spasmodic coughing, and the sound of a baby crying behind one of the eyeless windows.

"They're not bothering about us," whispered Josh.

"I don't think they can see us, Josh."

"D'you mean we're ghosts now, like Rosie?" Josh asked.

"I think we must be, we're in Rosie's time, I'm sure. Those men are Air Raid Wardens - and people used to call the Germans 'Jerries' during the war..."

"He called that a 'bombers' moon' - Beth, do you think...?"

"I don't think anything," snapped Bethan irritably. "I'm scared! I wish we hadn't come. Come on Josh - let's go back."

"No. Listen!"

"What?"

They strained their ears. There it was, a humming, a throbbing. The two A.R.P. wardens had heard it too.

"Ere we go," George sighed. "Come on mate."

As they moved off, the drone of heavy planes grew louder to be joined by the up-and-down wailing of the siren shrieking an air-raid warning. The siren stopped, the drone grew louder until it filled the air. The sky, already bright, was alive with moving paths of light, sweeping, criss-crossing, interlacing.

"Search lights!" breathed Joshua. Cracking and popping noises, like fireworks, could be heard in the distance.

"And guns!"

"Look!" Bethan's hand trembled as she pointed. From out of a huge bank of cloud swarmed a dark mass of planes, their shapes gleaming wet in the moonlight. The steady thrumbing noise became unbearable. The children pressed their hands to their ears and, fascinated, gazed skywards.

The explosion caught them unawares. They clasped each other, shocked and bewildered, as the buildings around them leapt into the air and crumbled and tumbled and folded to the ground.

Dust and smoke whirled around them. The drone of the planes, the screech of more bombs, the rat-a-tat of anti-aircraft guns, the grinding and crashing of masonry mingled in their heads with screams and shouts. A smell of gas accompanied more explosions, and fires started. Their smarting eyes peered through the haze. A plane fell out of the sky

pulling a trail of billowing black smoke behind it, then another. Turning as one, the planes returned the way they had come, the guns following them.

A new sound filled their ears. The all-clear siren. It's final whine merged with the clanging bells of fire-engines.

Rescue squads, A.R.P. wardens, Home Guard and anyone able to dig or lift set to work alongside the firemen. Volunteers arrived to help the injured.

People began to stagger, stumble, crawl from the rubble. Some had been lucky, and emerged dazed, but surprisingly cheerful - even cracking a joke or two. Others were hurt, some severely. A woman, hair in metal curlers, torn winceyette nightie clutched around her, wandered, bewildered, ignoring the blood streaming down her face. A younger woman, screaming hysterically, clutched at the arm of a rescue worker.

"'E's still in there, I tell yer. You've got ter get 'im out. Oh, Gawd! 'E's under all that lot! 'E went ter make a cuppa tea, see..."

"It's alright, luv, you show us where you think he is and we'll start digging." Pulling him to what had been her home, she fell to the ground and began to drag the debris away with her bare hands. Gently a neighbour led her away.

Gradually, carefully, injured and dead were carried out, to be greeted by tears of joy and relief, or wails of grief, or terrible, silent despair. Now and again the heaving, lifting and dragging would stop as everyone listened for some sound, a tapping, a cry. On hearing the slightest indication of life the rescuers would resume with increased energy. And all the while their efforts were threatened by falling walls and glass, explosions and fire.

Tears ran unchecked down the children's faces as they stood hand in hand, watching. The moon clouded over, darkening the once-brilliant night as if it didn't want them to see too much.

As if it, too, could not bear to look at such a terrible scene.

Chapter Eleven

The rescuers, slowing up now that a large number of people were accounted for, stopped for a steaming enamel mug of tea served by the W.V.S. from the back of a truck. Everyone was covered in a thick layer of whitish dust.

George's partner cleaned his glasses on his shirt-tail, pulled out of his waistband for the purpose, and, having adjusted them on his badly cut nose, reached into his shoulder-bag for a notebook and pencil. He looked around pityingly at the bewildered people sitting, lying, standing around him, some in groups, others in isolated numbness. This was the bit he hated most, when he had to write it down. Somehow it made it more real.

"Right! Number one. Everybody out?"

"Yeah. We're alright mate - just come out ter get a bit of air."

There was weak laughter as an entry was made in the notebook.

"Good! Number 3?"

"Missus is out - still looking for her old man." A choked cry, followed by reassuring noises greeted this announcement. Two entries this time, one on the page headed by a large red tick, the other on the page headed 'MISSING'.

"Number 5?" There was no response. "Number 5," he repeated, louder. "Nobody 'ere from number 5?"

"They were in - I heard them," the man from number 7 volunteered.

The warden turned to him, "Your lot all out?"

"Yes. Lucky the kids are out of the way - sent out little 'uns down the Tube with number fifteen's lot."

"So number fifteen's all accounted for too?"

"That's right - all down the Underground."

Numbers seven and fifteen were added to the first list. The columns lengthened.

"So we've got three more definites to get out - plus the whole family at number five. You're sure they were in? You don't think they could 'ave changed their minds and gone down the shelter at the last minute?"

"No - I heard them get up and come downstairs when the warning went. One of 'em was yelling - sounded as if he'd 'ad a wallop."

66

The warden nodded and looked across to where the house had been. That one had had a direct hit. No point hurrying - might as well finish his tea. Others were already back searching for those still missing, those that still had a chance.

The checking over, the blanket-wrapped survivors were helped into trucks to be taken to the rest centre set up in a nearby school. Ambulances took the injured to hospital.

Bethan and Joshua sat on a heap of rubble. The air was full of dust and it was hard to breathe. Acrid fumes filled their mouths and nostrils and there was still a strong smell of gas. On the corner of the street fire raged, unimpressed by the efforts of several fire-engines, the water from the heavy hoses appearing to do no more than push the fierce flames sideways, where lesser fires danced into life.

Occasionally, accompanied by a bang and a loud roar, a sheet of flame leapt skywards spraying sparks and falling debris, as escaping gas added to the terrifying spectacle.

As morning came a few people entered the street and stood quietly watching the rescuers as they tapped and called and dug and listened, still hoping for some sound from below the heaps of bricks and plaster and glass and the tangled mass of smashed furniture.

A boy came and stood silently facing the smouldering rubble-filled space where number five had been. He was about thirteen, small for his age, and had a wizened old-man-ish look. He stared blankly at the three men searching the ruins.

"Go on 'ome, Billy - there's nuthin' you can do 'ere." A motherly woman put her arm about his shoulders and tried to turn him away.

Bethan and Joshua looked at each other.

"It's Billy," Joshua whispered. Bethan nodded.

"Goin' out wi' me new Dad on the cart. Come ter get Rosie," he said, his speech slurred, indistinct. He opened his mouth wide between the words and his tongue seemed to get in the way. Small dribbles of

saliva trickled out and ran down one side of his chin, which he absentmindedly cuffed from time to time.

"Go on, Billy. It ain't no use 'anging about 'ere." One of the men straightened up, easing his back. "Go and tell your Mum the Jones' 'ave copped it. Good friends with Nellie Jones, your Mum was." He returned to the task of locating the family, but with no sense of urgency.

Billy stubbornly stood his ground, saying nothing, his eyes following the men.

"Over 'ere - give us 'and," one of them called. The other two came over and together they heaved a large hunk of wall to one side.

"Found the first of 'em," he answered gruffly.

Gently, carefully, as if afraid they could still hurt her, they carried the rag-doll child over the mounds of debris and laid her on a clear, flat patch of ground. As they lifted her, a kitten, marmalade fur grey and matted, eyes wild, leapt from beneath the lifeless body.

"Look at that! She saved the bleedin' cat." The man's voice was awed, admiring.

Billy had stood, unmoving, as his friend was lifted out. Only his eyes moved, and his fists, hanging by his sides on his over-long arms, clenched tightly. But as the kitten shot out of the hole, Billy darted

forwards, grabbing it before it had a chance
to run. Panic-stricken it spat and snarled
and scratched his face but Billy held it
firmly, talking to it, soothing it. With one
last look at Rosie, still murmuring to the
kitten held against his chest, he walked
away.

"Best thing," the motherly woman was
saying. " 'E thought the world of Rosie, and
she thought the world of that kitten. 'Er Dad
give it to 'er before 'e went orf to war. Told
'er ter look after it for 'im." She sniffed.
"Corse, 'e won't be back no more neiver," she
added.

Someone had covered Rosie with a coat
and the men returned to their painful,
gruesome work.

Bethan and Joshua stood a little apart from the small crowd, tears streaming down both white, drawn faces.

"Rosie," whispered Bethan. "Rosie. Please come back to us!" They turned blindly away, stumbling out of the street, and were startled to find themselves back in a night-shadowed neon-lit road, with the new moon glinting above the roof-tops.

Without a word, the same unspoken question in their minds, they took each other's hand and hesitantly tip-toed back to the corner. Drawing a deep breath they peeped around.

The street-lights gleamed yellow, casting long shadows. The tower blocks loomed larger than ever against a deep blue-velvet sky across which the first thin fingers of day reached out, as if to touch a star before it disappeared. The air, although not sweet with honeysuckle or hay or juniper as it was at home, was fresh and clean. No fumes, or thick, mouth-drying dust. No smell or taste of burning.

"It's gone," said Joshua unnecessarily. "As if it never happened."

"It happened," said Bethan.

Suddenly both children realized that they were very, very tired, and not a little frightened.

"Come on, Josh," said Bethan. "Let's get back."

The reassuring sound of gentle snoring greeted them as they quietly closed the flat door behind them. They remembered to put the chain on, and the keys back in their accustomed place.

Too weary to undress properly they dropped their shoes and top clothes in an untidy heap and fell into bed. The clock struck four.

"We haven't been gone long," murmured Bethan.

There was no answer from Joshua. He was already fast asleep.

Chapter Twelve

"Josh - wake up Josh! Nan called us ages ago." Bethan shook her young brother, who sat up reluctantly, knuckling his eyes. "Come on. We've got to hurry - in case Rosie comes back."

"S'posing she doesn't?"

"Well - at least we'll be there. It would be awful if she came and we didn't turn up."

"I s'pose so." He swung his legs over the side of the bed. "I've still got my track suit on," he commented, surprised.

"Yes - don't you remember? Last night?" She lowered her voice. Joshua remembered. He had thought for a moment - hoped - it had all been a dream.

"Alright," he said, hurrying now.

Rushing their breakfast, earning reproving looks from their grandparents, they dashed out. Bethan had wanted to talk to Nan about the previous night - but how could she without telling of their escapade? And who knew what punishment that would bring! They would be 'grounded' for sure, possibly taken home. And how could they help Rosie then? No, she decided, with a conspiratorial look at Joshua, they had better keep it to themselves. For the time being anyway.

"See you later, Nan, Grandpa - we're going to see if we can find Rosie." She grabbed Joshua's arm pulling him through the door as she spoke.

"Rosie?" queried Grandpa.

"A little friend they've made - round the corner - nice little girl," Nan cut in quickly, waving them off. Half-way down the stairs Bethan hesitated, then ran back. Nan was still standing in the doorway.

"Nan - could we have some of our money please - so we can get our own lunch - then we won't have to come back till this evening."

With the usual admonitions not to buy a lot of greasy food, to be sure to stay together, and to mind the roads, she waved them off once more.

With the money safely zipped into their jacket pockets, the children ran to Rosie's corner, slowing up only to cross Ladbroke Grove. Apart from the fact that it was very busy and therefore very dangerous, they knew that Louise Trevalyn would probably be watching from the flat window. At the corner they turned and waved, just in case.

Although it was only nine o'clock, the sun was already warm on their backs. The buildings stood out with stark clean lines against the clear sky. Just as the smaller, triangular rooftops had the previous night, lit by the full moon.

The 'bombers' moon'. They looked at each other and shivered.

There were a lot of people about. A group of young people, boys and girls, were sitting on, or lolling against, the wall. Their bit of wall - right where they wanted to be! Drawing nearer they could see there was no sign of Rosie.

"What are we going to do?" Bethan looked around, disappointed. "I was sure she would be here." She sounded tearful. Joshua looked at her keenly.

"You're not going to cry are you?" he asked anxiously. Biting her lip, she reassured him. Embarrassed, he might go back to the flat, leaving her alone. He probably didn't even remember he had cried with her last night. Or if he did he would never admit it.

The group moved off, chattering and laughing, pulling at each other. Hovering uncertainly until they were out of sight, the children ran to their accustomed place.

Rosie materialized before their eyes. A very pale, almost transparent Rosie. Only her sad hazel eyes looked solid. She smiled a weak, tired smile. Beth thought momentarily of the Cheshire Cat in 'Alice' and giggled nervously. Joshua was fascinated.

"Do that again!" he commanded. "Go on...let's see you do that trick again."

"Shut up, Josh," Bethan scolded. "Can't you see Rosie's..." she stopped, 'not well' didn't seem quite right. "Rosie's... she's tired."

"I'm getting weaker," her voice was small and thin. "I don't think I can stay much longer. They'll make me go back."

"Back where?"

"Where I was. But I don't want to go back there! I want to go where my mum and dad and Terry and Johnny are," her voice strengthened, but trembled with the effort.

"But why aren't you with them? You all... went... together - at least, you and your mum and your brothers did, so why did you split up?" Joshua was frowning with the effort of trying to work things out.

"They said I wasn't ready. Something was 'olding me. They said I'd 'ave a chance to find out what it was and put it right - then I can go on. But I'd 'ave ter wait fer the call."

"The call?" Both children spoke together.

"Yes. Someone 'ad ter call my name."

"And did they?" Beth sighed the words out, breathless with anticipation.

"Yes. But I don't know who - or why. And if I don't find out soon..." She trailed off and the three gazed ahead in troubled silence.

"Rosie," Bethan began gently. "Do you remember - that night?"

"Not really. I keep recalling bits - like I know now me Dad was killed - that's why 'e missed my birfday. But the night we was...no I don't remember that."

"Could you - bear to know about it?"

"Beth - I wanter know everyfing. Anyfing, what might 'elp me get to Mum and Dad."

So, quietly and gently, leaving nothing out, they told her, between them, of all they had seen and heard. Coming to the end of the story, Beth swallowed hard.

"As they lifted you, your cat - well a kitten really - ran out and Billy..."

"Tiger! 'E ran out? 'E didn't die? You're sure it was Tiger?"

"They said your dad gave him to you before he went overseas - a ginger stripy one."

"Dad said ter take care of 'im. Oh, I'm so glad 'e didn't die!" She looked stronger, her smile brighter, "I wonder what 'appened to 'im?"

"Billy took him."

Rosie placed her hand on Beth's arm and Beth was surprised to feel the grip, the pressure of the thin fingers.

"Beth, you must find Billy - find out what happened to Tiger."

"But how? We don't know where Billy went - or even if he's still alive. Nan didn't keep in touch with him."

"Please Beth - you must! They - the shadow people - didn't want me to come. They tried ter stop me - and now they keep tryin' ter pull me back. I told you - I ain't got much time. You've got ter find Billy!"

Chapter Thirteen

How were they to find him? They didn't even know his other name, and had not thought to ask Rosie before she left them.

"Let's start with the sweet shop," Bethan suggested. Nan had said she thought it was the same family who had it when she was a child. Of course the people she had seen serving were much younger, but the name was the same. At the mention of sweets Joshua, who, typically, had been raising objections, brightened.

"We'll have to buy something. Can't just go in and start asking questions." To his delight Bethan agreed.

"We'll buy ice-creams," she said.

A bell tinkled above the door as they entered. They asked for two Ninety-Nines and Bethan held out a one pound coin.

"There you are luvs," the young man passed the large cornets, each with a chocolate finger poised in its coiled and peaked mountain, over the counter. He smiled.

Pleased he seemed friendly, Bethan asked, "Your family lived here all through the war didn't they? My grandma used to live near here and we're trying to find some of her old friends. She remembers you."

"Not me luv! Wasn't even a twinkle in me dad's eye! My mum and granny and grandad were 'ere though. Perhaps Gran'll remember 'er. 'Ang on!"

Hopefully, they licked their ice-creams.

"Granny!" he shouted, pushing aside a beaded curtain and revealing a glimpse of a dark cluttered back room. "Gran! You're wanted."

An old lady, very fat, with wispy henna-dyed hair waddled into the shop on obviously painful legs. " 'Oo wants me?" She peered petulantly at the children. "Just 'avin a bit of a sit-down I was, bin on the go since five o'clock, sortin' out the papers. Can't leave the youngsters to do it all. They ain't got no go in 'em. 'Ad life too easy, if yer arsts me." She leaned heavily on the counter.

Her grandson grinned and pulled a face behind her back.

"Now then. What did yer want me fer?"

Bethan explained, with interruptions from Joshua, about Louise - Wee - Ashwood, and Rosie Jones and a boy called Billy. The old lady beamed, showing a few good teeth and a lot of gaps.

"Wee Ashwood! Remember 'er? I'll say I do!" She leaned towards them and, sighing heavily, enveloped them in her unpleasant, stale tobacco laden breath. They stepped back, just a little, trying not to be impolite.

"And poor little Rosie - never forget 'er, I won't. Nor them two cheeky little brothers of 'ers. Little tykes they was, 'tho' Rosie tried ter keep 'em in order. Great 'elp to 'er mum she was. Specially after they 'eard about 'er dad - got killed 'e did - France." She reached behind her for a stool and wriggled on to it, studying the children. "Well I never! Now I'm looking at yer proper I can see 'oo you are. Thought yer put me in mind o' someone! Went 'orf and married some country bloke she met when she was evacuated, Wee did. But poor Rosie - got killed, she did. Bombed, the lot of 'em. Last really bad night of the blitz, it was. Terrible night that was..."

The long-suffering look on her grandson's face told the children they were in for one of the old lady's regular recitals. Desperately, Bethan interrupted.

"What about Billy?"

"Billy?" The old lady, distracted from her usual routine, was confused for a moment. "Oh - Billy Dawson. Never saw 'im no more. No! Tell a lie. I did see 'im a couple o' times, on 'is dad's 'orse an' cart, but only passin'. Last I'd 'eard they'd given up totting and 'ad a stall down the Portabeller. Old junk and knick-knacks and stuff."

"Is that - Portobello Road?" Bethan asked absentmindedly nibbling the last of her ice-cream cornet.

"That's what I said - down the Portabeller. Your granny'll know it."

Thanking her, Bethan pulled Joshua towards the door. His ice-cream finished he was eyeing the sweets.

"Wait a minute. I 'aven't finished telling you..." She raised her voice as the children ran from the shop, forgetting to shut the door.

"Ask yer gran ter drop in," they heard above the still-tinkling bell.

They found Portobello Road without difficulty. Everyone knew the street market. It was crowded, and the breathless, impatient children had to slow their pace to a steady stroll. Weaving their way between people in every kind of dress, speaking in every language, they felt strange, as if they had stepped into another world. The smells wafting around them, perfumes and spices, 'take-aways' of every ethnic origin, beer and fruit and vegetables underlined the confusion of their eyes and ears. Loud music blared from shop doorways, and above it all, the cries of the costermongers and salesmen and women calling their wares. It seemed that everything, books, junk, second-hand clothing and furniture and food of every description, side-by-side with exquisite crafts and expensive antiques, was sold here.

But today they had no time to dawdle, to look and admire. Their queries about a man named Billy Dawson met with no success. Most of the stall-holders were from other areas and had only been there in recent times, since the market became popular with the tourists. Tired and disheartened, having walked all along one side and back the other, they returned to the lower, less fashionable end of the road. The now familiar local accent of a lady behind a vegetable stall attracted their attention. Hands on hips, she was talking to a small, thin man whose head, nodding in obvious approval, made him look like one of those car mascots.

"And I sez ter 'im, I sez 'my old dad 'ad this patch, man an' boy, fer fifty -odd years and I've 'ad it after 'im. And not you, nor some bleedin' jumped-up council bloke ain't

turnin' me orf it. ' Bloomin' cheek! Proper
liberty I calls it. But it'll take more then
them ter shift this barrer, I can tell yer."

She pushed her sleeves up revealing
strong, muscular arms, as if to take on
anyone who dared disagree with her.

"Please," Beth hesitated and cleared her
throat nervously.

"Go on," Joshua, fed-up, pushed his
sister forward. "Ask her."

"Excuse me - have you been here long?
I mean - during the war - when your father
had this stall? You see, we were wondering..."

She was cut off by a shriek of laughter.
"Cor - did you 'ear that? 'Ave I bin 'ere long?
Can a duck swim?" She laughed again,
making her chins and belly ripple and
wobble. "Did yer 'ear that, Bert?" She slapped
the little man hard on the shoulder, at which
he laughed too, a deep, throaty chuckle.

"You have been here a long time,"
Bethan persisted, taking this to mean 'yes'!

"Yes, I 'ave dearie - longer than I want
ter fink abart. 'Oo wants ter know?"

"I'm Bethan Trevalyn, and this is my
brother Joshua," Bethan replied politely.

"Oo!" The woman shrieked, laughing
again. "'Ark at 'er!" Trying to imitate
Bethan's round Cornish sounds she mimicked
the introduction.

"You ain't from round 'ere, that's fer
sure - not talkin' like that you ain't! She's

from the country, she is," she informed the small crowd which had gathered. "Come up from the sticks fer a bit 'o cultcher 'ave yer?" She slapped her great thigh with a resounding 'thwack!' and roared louder. Bethan, embarrassed, backed away.

"Give over, Lil. Leave the kid alone." Lil turned to the man and wiped her eyes.

"It's alright Bert, only my fun." She turned to the children. "What did yer want ter know? Not much goes on around 'ere that Big Lil don't know about."

"That's true." The man was nodding again, his neck wrinkled like a tortoise. "Proper oracle, our Lil."

"Did you know... Do you know a man called Billy? Billy Dawson? He used to have a barrow with ornaments and things."

"Billy Dawson? No, luv, ain't never bin no-one o' that name in the market. Sorry."

"Oh, but you must know him. He used to be in the market - I know he did! We've just got to find him."

Forgetting her nervousness Bethan rushed around the other side of the stall and looked up, pleading into the round, weather-beaten face. "Please think - try to remember! He was smallish, with thick glasses - and he spoke funny - and..."

"Oh - you mean Billy Watts - old Totter Watts' boy."

"Of course! We forgot his mother married again and he might have changed his name! Do you know him?" In her excitement Bethan gripped Joshua's hand hard. Frowning, he pulled away.

"Know Billy Watts? Course I knows 'im. We know Billy, don't we Bert?" The tortoise-head moved rapidly up and down.

"Then - please - can you tell us where to find him? It's very urgent. We've got to talk to him." Bethan, notebook and pencil in hand, waited hopefully for information.

"S'far as I know 'e ain't bin 'round 'ere lately - not since it went posh. Took 'is barrer and got space over the Bush, Shepherd's Bush Market - Gold'awk Road end."

"Is it far? Can you tell us how to get there?"

"No - t'ain't far." The children sighed audibly with relief. "Tube from Ladbroke Grove's quickest. Get out at Gold'awk Road and you're there."

Hugging the surprised woman and grabbing Joshua Bethan ran towards the Underground station.

"Well, I'll be blowed," the woman exclaimed. "Whatever could they want wiv ole Billy?"

Chapter Fourteen

It had been frightening, but exciting too, travelling on the Underground alone. Luckily there were not too many people about, so they were not hustled forward as they had been in the centre of the city. They stood well back on the platform and held their breath as the fast, grey monster thundered in. They only just got in before the automatic doors closed catching Joshua's anorak in their grip. Partially opening to release him, they snapped shut again and the train hurtled forward, throwing the children from side to side as they made their way to a seat.

It was hot and stuffy in the carriage, and smelt of sweat and garlic and a mixture of perfumes and hair-sprays. Some lads at the far end had their feet on the opposite seat, earning disapproving looks from other passengers. But nobody said anything.

It was only a couple of stops to Goldhawk Road - all overground, causing Joshua to argue all the way that they hadn't been on the Underground at all! Finding the market had been easy and tracking Billy down had been easy too. The very first stall-holder, a big bear-like friendly man had directed them to this tall, narrow, grey house where, he said, Billy Watts lived.

"Ain't bin too well for a couple of weeks, poor ole Billy," the man had informed them, coming round to the front of his stall, leaving a sulky-looking girl putting out more stock. "'Is chest ketchin' up wiv 'im. Always was weak in the chest. An' course, since 'is mum an' dad popped orf 'e ain't 'ad no-one ter look after 'im proper; an' 'e won't let no-one else 'elp 'im. Independent buggar -'scuse my French." He put a large hairy arm companionably around each child and, leaving his stall, edged them through the crowds. "Yer see that geezer there, wiv Mickey Mouse Balloons? Well, yer go past 'im and keep on till yer come ter the cockle an' whelk stall. Just past 'im there's a bit of an alley. Cut through there and Billy's 'ouse is dead opposite - number one-seven-nine. 'E's got a room down in the basement."

Bethan wrote the instructions in her notebook.

"Sure you'll be alright now?" They assured him they would. "In that case I'll get back. Our Debbie's not 'appy left on the stall. Rather be at 'ome watchin' the telly an' doin' 'er nails. Just like 'er muvver!" He laughed, an affectionate, tolerant laugh and, waving away their thanks, bulldozed his way back to his corner pitch.

Four minutes later they stood outside number 179. There were four storeys above ground, a steep flight of steps leading up to the front door, and an even steeper flight twisting down to the basement, below pavement level.

Somebody had once tried to turn the area into a little courtyard. Bits of rusted chain, once used to hold potted plants, hung from nails sticking out of the brick. The drunken remains of a window-box teetered precariously on the once-white, near ground level, window sill. The door, once painted a shiny black, was peeling, revealing patches of brown chocolate. The lower window-panes were cracked and, through the thick layers of grime a blanket could be seen, draped across in place of a curtain.

The bell didn't work, so Bethan knocked on the door, waited, then knocked again, louder. There was no sound from within. Bethan, hesitantly turned the handle and the door creaked open, tilting slightly as a hinge pulled away.

"Mr Watts... Billy... are you there?" Bethan was nervous and her voice sounded strange. Joshua looked at her accusingly. "You're scared!"

"No I'm not! It's just... well... a bit creepy, that's all," Bethan whispered.

"I'm not scared," Joshua said loudly, boldly. But he kept behind Bethan as they crept slowly along the narrow dark passage. "Anyway," he added "we've left the door open, so we can always scat off if we're worried."

"We're not going to scat - we're going to find Billy," Bethan hissed fiercely. She didn't feel very brave, but she knew they had to go on. Midway along the passage two doors stood together. Wondering which one was Billy's, Bethan tapped gently on the first door. There was movement, but no reply.

"There's someone in there - I heard someone," Bethan had her hand on the door-handle. Joshua pulled at her arm.

"Come on Beth, let's go. It's horrible in here."

But Bethan had opened the door and was peeping in. The room was dark and gloomy. Two thin rays of sunshine picked their way through the tattered window-cover and crept over the bare concrete floor towards the bed in the far corner, not quite reaching it. A stale, sour smell filled their nostrils and, for a moment or two, they held their breath.

"Billy?" Bethan cautiously approached what looked like a mound of clothes on the bed. "Billy?"

The mound moved and a face emerged. Even in the gloom they could see it was an ill face. It was deathly-white except for a bright spot on each cheek. The eyes, sunk back into the head, were feverish and bright, the lips dry, scaly, with little sores around the mouth and nose. Struggling to sit up the face was followed by a scarf-wrapped neck then an upper body, thick with jumpers, under which a rattling chest rumbled and wheezed. The effort of moving brought a prolonged bout of coughing. A tumbler stood on the floor beside the bed, and beside it, a milk bottle; none too clean, half-filled with water. Bethan poured a little into the glass and held it out.

"Here, Billy. You are Billy Watts aren't you?"

He nodded, closing his hands around the glass and sipping carefully. They waited for him to get his breath back.

"Billy - you're ill - you should go to hospital."

"Don't - like - 'orspitals," Billy whined. "Don't let 'em take me to 'orspital."

"No - alright. Not if you don't want to go," Bethan promised hastily, afraid he might start coughing again. Taking the glass and putting it back on the floor she sat gingerly on the edge of the bed, motioning Joshua to do the same.

She didn't know what to say, how to begin. Would he still remember Nan? And Rosie? Would bringing back old memories upset him? He really did look very ill.

She looked up. He was watching her, his head on one side, reminding her of the robin at home. She flushed as he continued to stare at her, and wriggled uncomfortably.

"I'm sorry - just coming in like this. We did knock."

"You Wee's little girl? Look like Wee you do!"

"No - well - yes, in a way. She's my grandmother."

"And mine," put in Joshua.

"You ain't like 'er," Billy said dismissively.

"Billy," Bethan spoke gently, putting her hand over his as it rested on the covers. "Do you remember Rosie?" She was distressed to see Billy's eyes fill with tears.

"Rosie. Went ter take 'er out..."

"We know. You looked after her cat. Tiger. What happened to Tiger, Billy?" She stopped, unsure how much to tell him. "She - I'm sure she would want to know," she finished lamely.

To the childrens' dismay Billy burst into loud, choking sobs.

"I tried t'tell 'er. Went round 'er street - but it'd all gone. Then I got me mum and dad ter take me up the cemetery - but she wasn't there either. They said she was there - 'ad 'er name on an' everthin' - but she wasn't. Then we went round her church - put a candle up for the Jones', me mum wanted ter do that, 'cos of 'er and Rosie's mum bein' friends. But she said it wouldn't do Rosie no good. She said Rosie'd want ter know about Tiger before she'd settle down. I wish I could 'a' told 'er, but I didn't know 'ow to."

They sat patiently through another bout of coughing and Billy wiped his eyes on his scarf.

"We know how to tell her, Billy - tell us, please." But Billy, exhausted, had fallen back, mouth open, eyes half-closed.

"I think we'd better let him rest a bit," Bethan whispered to Joshua.

"What do we do - just sit here?" Joshua wanted to know.

"No - let's tidy the place up. And perhaps we can find a kitchen - make him a nice cup of tea."

Joshua pulled a face, but obediently began to help. "Wish it was a bit lighter in here," Joshua complained.

"So do I," Bethan agreed.

There was no bulb in the light. They decided to move the blanket covering the window down a bit. If they fixed it half-way nobody could see in.

Positioning a chair on each side they unhooked the holey, grey army blanket. Clouds of dust arose, dancing in the sudden sunlight. They sneezed. Carrying it between them they took it outside into the air and gave it a good shake as they had seen their mother do at home. They couldn't remove the nails that had held it in place, but found a strip of coiled wire still stretched across the bottom half of the window, where once a net curtain had been.

"This'll do," said Bethan, tucking the blanket over evenly. "Can't see the holes now, either."

They could see across the room clearly now. The walls, emulsioned a pale green, were bare except for a wooden crucifix and a picture-postcard of a seaside resort stuck up with blue-tack. But the feeling of space was lost as soon as they took their eyes from the walls. Everywhere else, floor, mantlepiece, chairs, chest-of-drawers, was submerged in clutter. Dirty mugs, some with green mould growing on the dregs, stood on or under magazines and newspapers. The magazines had been bought for the pictures of horses on the covers, some of which had been cut out. The newspapers had mostly been used to wrap fish and chips. On an armchair, under an old coat, they found a saddle and various pieces of horse tack; a pile of horse brasses made a 'leaning tower of Pisa' in the hearth. There were a number of shoes and boots, some with holes in the bottom, which they paired up and stood in a row under the window. Bethan found a piece of cloth and went around the room wiping off as much dust as she could, putting clothes and papers in neat piles on chairs as she went.

"There - that's better," she said, looking round with some satisfaction. "Now, let's see if we can find somewhere to wash these up." She picked up several mugs and Joshua followed with two more.

In a scullery at the far end of the passage they found a sink. They washed up in cold water - the gas heater over the sink looked old and complicated and they decided not to risk using it. The electric kettle didn't work either, but they discovered a small milk-pan in a cupboard, and boiled some water on the gas stove. There were two tea-bags and a cup of sugar on a shelf, but no milk.

Bethan made a mug of strong, sweet tea and carried the dark, steaming liquid into the front room. Billy was stirring. He seemed better after the tea and Bethan asked again about Tiger. Billy pointed to the chest of drawers.

"Photos in there - bottom drawer."

The drawer was crammed with photograph albums and piles and packets of photographs.

'Goodness,' thought Bethan, 'we'll never have time to go through all of these!' She was getting worried about the time already.

"Blue envelope," Billy was saying, struggling to get out of bed. He was fully dressed except for his shoes.

"No, stay there Billy, you're not well enough. We'll find it," Bethan said firmly, handing a pile from the drawer to Joshua.

"Here it is," he held up a grubby faded blue envelope, then took it across and placed it in Billy's outstretched hand. Billy sat holding it for what seemed a long time.

"Billy," Bethan prompted. "Tiger."

Slowly Billy opened the envelope and withdrew an old black and white photograph. It was of a very large, light-coloured cat, faintly striped, sitting on a cushion. Beside it was a Christmas stocking out of which a toy mouse peeped. On the back was written 'Tiger. Xmas 1956.'

"That was 'is last Christmas," said Billy. "'E died a few months later - goin' on sixteen 'e was." His eyes filled with tears again.

"Don't cry, Billy. May we borrow this picture? I promise you'll get it back. Rosie will be so happy." Bethan was anxious now to be off. She was afraid they may still not be in time to help Rosie - she had said she had only a little time left.

But how could they leave Billy? The stall-holder had said he wouldn't let anyone help him, yet in many ways he was like a child. She had an idea.

"Billy - you've done something really special for Rosie - taking such good care of Tiger. Would you do one more thing for her?"

"Rosie - ain't nothin' I wouldn't do for Rosie."

"Billy - Rosie wants you to get better - to go to work in the market again." He nodded eagerly. "Well - to do that, first you'll have to have the doctor - he'll give you some medicine. He might even want you to go to - hospital - just for a little while." Billy, who had been smiling and nodding, now looked agitated.

"No - no 'orspital."

He explained slowly, breathing and talking with difficulty, how a couple of weeks ago he had been admitted to hospital after a fall. "Knocked meself out I did, and when I came round a nasty nurse told me off. Said I was waking everyone up, shouting for Rosie. Wasn't my fault. I never knew I was shouting."

Bethan reassured him, telling him that most nurses are kind. She spoke automatically, her mind not on what she was saying, but on what Billy had just said.

'I was waking them all up, shouting for Rosie.'

And in her head, a small voice saying 'I had to wait for the call.'

Urgently she leaned forward. "Billy. We've got to go. Please let us get you a doctor. We can't leave you like this."

"No 'orspital." Billy sunk down into the bundle of covers. Then Bethan remembered something. Of course!

"Billy, our nan - Wee - was a nurse."

Billy's head poked up again.

"Wee - a nurse?"

"That's right - for years and years. And she's lovely, hardly ever cross," she sat still, smiling encouragingly.

Billy gave her his long strange stare. Then he nodded. "Dr Waters, on corner. Me mum used ter 'ave 'im."

Later, after a severe scolding for being so late and an even more severe one when their grandparents learned where they had been, the children sat in bed talking.

"We must go as early as possible in the morning," Bethan said. "We've got to get to Rosie in time."

Joshua suggested she might be gone already, but Bethan's spirits were not to be dampened. She was sure they would see their friend again.

Chapter Fifteen

"Now, I want a promise from you two, that you will not go out of this area today - do you hear?" Nan's face was stern. The promise made, they escaped into the street.

"Whew! I thought she wasn't going to let us out!"

"She wouldn't Josh, except she knows we've got to see Rosie."

They both felt sad and uncomfortable. Their grandparents had never been so angry with them before. Of course they had been glad they had found Billy, but cross with them for going on their own. Nan had immediately rung Dr Waters, and Grandpa had sat shaking his head, commenting that they had all been 'put in with the cakes and took out with the buns'. Even his usually solid, sensible Wee was talking about a ghost-child!

They were approaching the corner and Bethan's face grew solemn. She had been so sure Rosie would be there, so certain that all their efforts to help their friend would be successful. But now? With just two more steps to go, she stopped, afraid. Supposing Rosie wasn't there? Supposing the shadow-people had already clawed her back?

Condemning her to spend forever in a no-mans-land, tied to the earth, unable to get free to join her parents and brothers? And if that happened how could she, Bethan, bear it, knowing that she had the key to release her? Here, in the blue envelope in her hand.

"Josh," she put her hand out to her brother, her voice quaking. "Josh - I can't go on. You look...please." She gave him a gentle push forward. "Tell me - tell me if she's there."

The moment that followed seemed so long! Bethan stood, frozen, as Joshua, seemingly in slow motion, peered around the corner. He turned back towards Bethan.

She's not there! The thought raced through Bethan's head, making her feel weak and her knees shake.

"Yes. She's there." Joshua's words were for a moment, unbelievable.

"She's there? Are you sure?"

"'Course I'm sure. See for yourself."

Rosie was sitting on the wall.

"Rosie!" Bethan's lead-heavy legs grew light as she flew along the street, Joshua, for once, trailing behind her.

"Rosie. Oh, Rosie!"

Rosie was slumped, listless and resigned. On hearing her name she lifted her head slowly. Her eyes, tired and dull, rested first on Bethan, then Joshua, then back to Bethan.

"You didn't find Billy then." It wasn't a question. "Well, it's too late now! I can't 'old on no longer. I'll 'ave ter go. Fanks anyway." She began to fade.

"No - Rosie. No! Wait! We did find Billy! And look!" Fumbling she withdrew the photograph from its envelope. "Look! It's Tiger! Billy had him - 'til he was really old - sixteen. Nan - Wee - says that's a good age for a cat. And you can see he's fine. Billy loved him. And he loved you too, he's been calling for you." She was gabbling, thrusting the photograph towards Rosie, expecting any moment that Rosie would disappear completely - forever.

But Rosie was getting stronger! Within a minute or two she was as they had seen her first, an ordinary-looking girl, a bit pale, but with bright, sparkling, laughing eyes.

"You did it!"

"Yes - we did alright, didn't we?" Joshua was proud of his part in the adventure.

"We did alright," Bethan agreed.

Rosie was looking at the photograph. "I didn't get yer killed, did I! I thought I 'ad." She looked at her friends. "You see, 'e wanted ter go out, an' I wouldn't let 'im - made 'im stop in wiv me." She lowered her eyes to the photograph again.

"Look at yer, yer great fat lump! Lived the life of Riley by the looks of it!"

They sat for a while, Bethan and Joshua telling of the previous day, and how Nan and Grandpa were going to keep an eye on Billy.

Rosie continued to gaze at Tiger.

"Can I keep this, just for today?" she asked.

Bethan explained they were to go home tomorrow.

"But we'll come in the morning - early - to say goodbye - we can collect it then and post it to Billy."

"Alright," agreed Rosie with a smile.

They were just about to climb on to the wall to wait - half and hour, Nan had said, not a moment longer - when the blue envelope fluttered to the ground at Bethan's feet. She picked it up, turning it over and over in her hands.

"She's not coming Josh. She's gone!"

"She didn't even say goodbye," Joshua was disappointed. He was getting used to having a ghost for a friend, even if it was a girl.

"Yes she did, Josh. Look." Bethan was examining the wall closely. Written into the red brick with scratchy white letters was:

'Bye and thanks. Love Rosie.'

In silence the children walked away. Once, before turning the corner, they looked back, seeing the tall grey tower block, the long low red-brick wall; remembering a street with rows of little houses.

"Goodbye, Rosie," Bethan whispered.

Reaching the main road, Joshua went to turn right, towards the flat. They would be leaving in less than an hour. Bethan turned the other way and began to walk hurriedly towards the Halfpenny steps.

"Where we going?" Joshua asked.

Bethan reached into her pocket and took out a coin.

"We're going to light a candle for Rosie."

Printed in the United Kingdom
by Lightning Source UK Ltd.
123734UK00001B/147/A